M O L Y
and
My Sad Captains

MOLY

AND

My Sad Captains

THOM GUNN

FARRAR, STRAUS AND GIROUX   NEW YORK

Second printing, 1977

First American edition of *Moly*, 1973
Printed in the United States of America
Designed by Pat de Groot

ACKNOWLEDGMENTS

These poems first appeared in the following publications: *Ambit, Antaeus, Art and Artists, Carleton Miscellany, Critical Quarterly, Encounter, Free You, Listen, The Listener, London Magazine, Observer, Paris Review, Poetry, Poetry Review, Southern Review,* and *Tri Quarterly.* Some were broadcast on the BBC and some appeared in pamphlets published by the Albondocani Press, Richard Gilbertson, the Pym-Randall Press, and the Sycamore Press. "The Messenger," "Being Born," and "The Discovery of the Pacific" were first published in *Poetry.* "Rites of Passage," "For Signs," "Justin," and "Words" were first published in *Southern Review.*

CONTENTS

MOLY

Rites of Passage   5
Moly   6
For Signs   8
Justin   10
Phaedra in the Farm House   11
The Sand Man   13
Apartment Cats   14
Three   15
Words   17
From the Wave   18
Tom-Dobbin   20
The Rooftop   23
The Color Machine   25
Street Song   27
The Fair in the Woods   29
Listening to Jefferson Airplane   31
To Natty Bumppo   32
The Garden of the Gods   33
Flooded Meadows   35
Grasses   36
The Messenger   37
Being Born   38

At the Center   40

The Discovery of the Pacific   43

Sunlight   44

My Sad Captains

PART ONE

In Santa Maria del Popolo   51

The Annihilation of Nothing   53

The Monster   54

The Middle of the Night   56

Readings in French   58

From the Highest Camp   60

Innocence   61

Modes of Pleasure   62

Modes of Pleasure   63

A Map of the City   64

The Book of the Dead   65

The Byrnies   67

Black Jackets   69

Baudelaire among the Heroes   71

The Value of Gold   72

Claus von Stauffenberg   73

PART TWO

Waking in a Newly Built House   77

Flying above California   78

Considering the Snail   79
"Blackie, the Electric Rembrandt"   80
Hotblood on Friday   81
The Feel of Hands   82
L'Épreuve   83
Rastignac at 45   84
Lights among Redwood   86
Adolescence   87
A Trucker   88
Loot   89
My Sad Captains   91

MOLY

for Mike and Bill,
with love

When I was near the house of Circe, I met Hermes in the likeness of a young man, the down just showing on his face. He came up to me and took my hand, saying: 'Where are you going, alone, and ignorant of the way? Your men are shut up in Circe's sties, like wild boars in their lairs. But take heart, I will protect you and help you. Here is a herb, one of great virtue: keep it about you when you go to Circe's house.' As he spoke he pulled the herb out of the ground and showed it to me. The root was black, the flower was as white as milk; the gods call it Moly.

Rites of Passage

Something is taking place.
Horns bud bright in my hair.
My feet are turning hoof.
And Father, see my face
—Skin that was damp and fair
Is barklike and, feel, rough.

See Greytop how I shine.
I rear, break loose, I neigh
Snuffing the air, and harden
Towards a completion, mine.
And next I make my way
Adventuring through your garden.

My play is earnest now.
I canter to and fro.
My blood, it is like light.
Behind an almond bough,
Horns gaudy with its snow,
I wait live, out of sight.

All planned before my birth
For you, Old Man, no other,
Whom your groin's trembling warns.
I stamp upon the earth
A message to my mother.
And then I lower my horns.

Moly

Nightmare of beasthood, snorting, how to wake.
I woke. What beasthood skin she made me take?

Leathery toad that ruts for days on end,
Or cringing dribbling dog, man's servile friend,

Or cat that prettily pounces on its meat,
Tortures it hours, then does not care to eat:

Parrot, moth, shark, wolf, crocodile, ass, flea.
What germs, what jostling mobs there were in me.

These seem like bristles, and the hide is tough.
No claw or web here: each foot ends in hoof.

Into what bulk has method disappeared?
Like ham, streaked. I am gross—grey, gross, flap-eared.

The pale-lashed eyes my only human feature.
My teeth tear, tear. I am the snouted creature

That bites through anything, root, wire, or can.
If I was not afraid I'd eat a man.

Oh a man's flesh already is in mine.
Hand and foot poised for risk. Buried in swine.

I root and root, you think that it is greed,
It is, but I seek out a plant I need.

Direct me, gods, whose changes are all holy,
To where it flickers deep in grass, the moly:

Cool flesh of magic in each leaf and shoot,
From milky flower to the black forked root.

From this fat dungeon I could rise to skin
And human title, putting pig within.

I push my big grey wet snout through the green,
Dreaming the flower I have never seen.

For Signs

In front of me, the palings of a fence
Throw shadows hard as board across the weeds;
The cracked enamel of a chicken bowl
Gleams like another moon; each clump of reeds
Is split with darkness and yet bristles whole.
The field survives, but with a difference.

And sleep like moonlight drifts and clings to shape.
My mind, which learns its freedom every day,
Sinks into vacancy but cannot rest.
While moonlight floods the pillow where it lay,
It walks among the past, weeping, obsessed,
Trying to master it and learn escape.

I dream: the real is shattered and combined,
Until the moon comes back into that sign
It stood in at my birth-hour; and I pass
Back to the field where, statued in the shine,
Someone is gazing upward from the grass
As if toward vaults that honeycomb the mind.

Slight figure in a wide black hat, whose hair
Massed and moon-colored almost hides his face.
The thin white lips are dry, the eyes intense

Watching not thing, but lunar orgy, chase,
Trap, and cool fantasy of violence.
I recognize the pale long inward stare.

His tight young flesh is only on the top.
Beneath it is an answering moon, at full,
Pitted with craters and with empty seas.
Dream mentor, I have been inside that skull,
I too have used those cindered passages.

But now the moon leaves Scorpio: I look up.

3

No, not inconstant, though it is called so.
For I have always found it waiting there,
Whether reduced to an invisible seed,
Or whether swollen again above the air
To rake the oubliettes of pain and greed
Opened at night in fellowship below.

It goes, and in its going it returns,
Cycle that I in part am governed by
And cannot understand where it is dark.
I lean upon the fence and watch the sky,
How light fills blinded socket and chafed mark.
It soars, hard, full, and edged, it coldly burns.

9

Justin

Waiting for her in some small park,
The lamplight's little world clasped round
By sweet rot and the autumn dark,
Once Justin found, or thought he found,
His live flesh flake like onion-skin
From finger-bones where it had held,
And saw the muscle fray within,
Peeling from joints that bunched and swelled.
    The waits had totalled in the shade,
And he had, unaware of debt
Or of expense, already paid
The cost of what he didn't get.
Might she be there? He could not see.
But waiting wears as hard as action,
And he perceived what he would be,
Transparent with dissatisfaction.

Phaedra in the Farm House

From sleep, before first light,
I hear slow-rolling churns
Clank over flags below.
Aches me. The room returns.
I hurt, I wake, I know
The cold dead end of night.

Here father. And here son.
What trust I live between.
But warmth here on the sheet
Is kin-warmth, slow and clean.
I cook the food two eat,
But oh, I sleep with one.

And you, in from the stable.
You spent last evening
Lost in the chalky blues
Of warm hills, rabbitting.
You frown and spell the news,
With forearms on the table.

Tonight, though, we play cards.
You are not playing well.
I smell the oil-lamp's jet,
The parlor's polished smell,
Then you—soap, ghost of sweat,
Tractor oil, and the yards.

Shirt-sleeved you concentrate.
Your moleskin waistcoat glints.
Your quick grin never speaks:
I study you for hints
—Hints from those scrubbed boy-cheeks?

I deal a grown man's fate.

The churns wait on in mud:
Tomorrow's milk will sour.
I leave, but bit by bit,
Sharp through the last whole hour.
The chimney will be split,
And that waistcoat be blood.

The Sand Man

Tourists in summer, looking at the view,
    The Bay, the Gate, the Bridge,
From sands that, yearly, city trucks renew,
    Descry him at the postcard's edge.

A white-haired man who hauls up lengths of wood
    And lies beside his fire
Motionless on his side, or gumming food,
    Without a thought, or much desire.

After the beating, thirty-five years since,
    A damaged consciousness
Reduced itself to that mere innocence
    Many have tried to repossess.

Bare to the trunks, the body on the ground
    Is sun-stained, ribbed, and lean:
And slowly in the sand rolls round and round
    In patient reperformed routine.

Sand, sticking to him, keeps him from the dust,
    And armors him about.
Now covered, he has entered that old trust,
    Like sandflies when the tide is out.

He rocks, a blur on ridges, pleased to be.
    Dispersing with the sands
He feels a dry cool multiplicity
    Gilding his body, feet and hands.

Apartment Cats

The Girls wake, stretch, and pad up to the door.
    They rub my leg and purr:
    One sniffs around my shoe,
    Rich with an outside smell,
  The other rolls back on the floor—
White bib exposed, and stomach of soft fur.

Now, more awake, they re-enact Ben Hur
    Along the corridor,
    Wheel, gallop; as they do,
    Their noses twitching still,
  Their eyes get wild, their bodies tense,
Their usual prudence seemingly withdraws.

And then they wrestle: parry, lock of paws,
    Blind hug of close defense,
    Tail-thump, and smothered mew.
    If either, though, feel claws,
  She abruptly rises, knowing well
How to stalk off in wise indifference.

Three

All three are bare.
The father towels himself by two grey boulders
   Long body, then long hair,
Matted like rainy bracken, to his shoulders.

   The pull and risk
Of the Pacific's touch is yet with him:
   He kicked and felt it brisk,
Its cold live sinews tugging at each limb.

   It haunts him still:
Drying his loins, he grins to notice how,
   Struck helpless with the chill,
His cock hangs tiny and withdrawn there now.

   Near, eyes half-closed,
The mother lies back on the hot round stones,
   Her weight to theirs opposed
And pressing them as if they were earth's bones.

   Hard bone, firm skin,
She holds her breasts and belly up, now dry,
   Striped white where clothes have been,
To the heat that sponsors all heat, from the sky.

   Only their son
Is brown all over. Rapt in endless play,
   In which all games make one,
His three-year nakedness is everyday.

Swims as dogs swim.
Rushes his father, wriggles from his hold.
    His body, which is him,
Sturdy and volatile, runs off the cold.

    Runs up to me:
Hi there hi there, he shrills, yet will not stop,
    For though continually
Accepting everything his play turns up

    He still leaves it
And comes back to that pebble-warmed recess
    In which the parents sit,
At watch, who had to learn their nakedness.

Words

The shadow of a pine-branch quivered
On a sunlit bank of pale unflowering weed.
I watched, more solid by the pine,
The dark exactitude that light delivered,
And, from obsession, or from greed,
Labored to make it mine.

In looking for the words, I found
Bright tendrils, round which that sharp outline faltered:
Limber detail, no bloom disclosed.
I was still separate on the shadow's ground
But, charged with growth, was being altered,
Composing uncomposed.

From the Wave

It mounts at sea, a concave wall
   Down-ribbed with shine,
And pushes forward, building tall
   Its steep incline.

Then from their hiding rise to sight
   Black shapes on boards
Bearing before the fringe of white
   It mottles toward.

Their pale feet curl, they poise their weight
   With a learn'd skill.
It is the wave they imitate
   Keeps them so still.

The marbling bodies have become
   Half wave, half men,
Grafted it seems by feet of foam
   Some seconds, then,

Late as they can, they slice the face
   In timed procession:
Balance is triumph in this place,
   Triumph possession.

The mindless heave of which they rode
   A fluid shelf
Breaks as they leave it, falls and, slowed,
   Loses itself.

Clear, the sheathed bodies slick as seals
   Loosen and tingle;
And by the board the bare foot feels
   The suck of shingle.

They paddle in the shallows still;
   Two splash each other;
Then all swim out to wait until
   The right waves gather.

Tom-Dobbin

centaur poems

1

light is in the pupil
                    luminous seed
and light is in the mind
                    crossing
in an instant
                    passage between the two
seamless
            imperceptible transition
skin melting downward into hide
at the centaur's waist
                        there is the one
and at once it is also the other

fair freckled skin, the blond down on it
being at all points
                a beginning
to the glossy chestnut brown which
is also at all points
                    a beginning upward

2

Hot in his mind, Tom watches Dobbin fuck,
Watches, and smiles with pleasure, oh what luck.
He sees beyond, and knows he sees, red cows,

Harsh green of grass, and pink-fired chestnut boughs.
The great brown body rears above the mare,
Plunging beneath Tom's interested stare.

In coming Tom and Dobbin join to one—
Only a moment, just as it is done:
A shock of whiteness, shooting like a star,
In which all colors of the spectrum are.

3

He grins, he plunges into orgy. It moves about
him in easy eddies, and he enters their mingling
and branching. He spreads with them, he is veined
with sunshine.
    The cobalt gleam of a peacock's neck, the course
of a wind through grasses, distant smoke frozen in
the sky, are extensions of self.
    And later something in him rises, neither sun nor
moon, close and brilliant. It lights the debris, and
brings it all together. It grins too, with its own
concentrating passion. It discovers dark shining
tables of rock that rise, inch by inch, out of the
turning waters.

4

The mammal is with her young. She is unique.
Millions of years ago mixed habits gave
That crisp perfected outline, webs, fur, beak.

Risen from her close tunnel to her cave
The duck-billed platypus lies in ripeness till
The line of her belly breaks into a dew.
The brown fur oozes milk for the young one. He,
Hatched into separation, beaks his fill.
If you could see through darkness you could see
One breaking outline that includes the two.

5

Ruthlessly gentle, gently ruthless we move
As if through water with delaying limb.
We circle clasping round an unmarked center
Gradually closing in, until we enter
The haze together—which is me, which him?
Selves floating in the one flesh we are of.

The Rooftop

White houses bank the hill,
Facing me where I sit.
It should be adequate
To watch the gardens fill

With sunlight, washing tree,
Bush, and the year's last flowers,
And to sit here for hours,
Becoming what I see.

Perception gave me this:
A whole world, bit by bit.
Yet I cannot grasp it—
Bits, not an edifice.

Long webs float on the air.
Glistening, they fall and lift.
I turn it down, the gift:
Such fragile lights can tear.

The heat frets earth already,
Harrowed by furious root;
The wireworm takes his loot;
The midday sun is steady.

Petals turn brown and splay:
Loose in a central shell
Seeds whitening dry and swell
Which light fills from decay.

Ruthless in clean unknowing
The plant obeys its need,
And works alone. The seed
Bursts, bare as bone in going,

Bouncing from rot toward earth,
Compound of rot, to wait,
An armored concentrate
Containing its own birth.

An unseen edifice.
The seen, the tangles, lead
From seed to death to seed
Through green closed passages.

The light drains from the hill.
The gardens rustle, cold,
Huddled in dark, and hold,
Waiting for when they fill.

The Color Machine

for Mike Caffee

1

Suddenly it is late night, there are people
in the basement, we all sit and lie in front of the
color machine. Someone among us, at the controls,
switches to green and red. Now the shape in it is
riding through a dark red-green sea, it is like matter
approaching and retreating from the brink of form.
Where it has thickened it starts to turn transparent;
where it is almost transparent it starts to thicken.
We cannot tell what it reminds us of: it is in a state
of unending alteration: we can name it only afterwards.

2

Giving himself completely to the color machine,
one of us became invisible. Being a thing, it does not
need gifts, and anyway what wants something that
becomes invisible as soon as given? It let him go, and he
drifted from the room into a world where he could no
longer make an impression: plants grew into the bridge
of his foot, cars drove through him, he entered movies for
free. And of course, we never saw him again.
I too am a lover, but I am cowardly, selfish, and
calculating. When I most long to give myself, heart,
body, and mind, to the color machine, I remember our
friend, give a mocking smile, and start making love to

curtains. By means of such promiscuity I can keep myself intact. But I am uneasy, and hanker for courage and impulsiveness. Perhaps, for our vanished friend, the moment of giving made the fact of his disintegration something of negligible importance. Or perhaps his consciousness still lives in the intensity of that moment. I am visible and do not know.

1965

Street Song

I am too young to grow a beard
But yes man it was me you heard
In dirty denim and dark glasses.
I look through everyone who passes
But ask him clear, I do not plead,
Keys lids acid and speed.

My grass is not oregano.
Some of it grew in Mexico.
You cannot guess the weed I hold,
Clara Green, Acapulco Gold,
Panama Red, you name it man,
Best on the street since I began.

My methedrine, my double-sun,
Will give you two lives in your one,
Five days of power before you crash.
At which time use these lumps of hash
—They burn so sweet, they smoke so smooth,
They make you sharper while they soothe.

Now here, the best I've got to show,
Made by a righteous cat I know.
Pure acid—it will scrape your brain,
And make it something else again.
Call it heaven, call it hell,
Join me and see the world I sell.

Join me, and I will take you there,
Your head will cut out from your hair
Into whichever self you choose.
With Midday Mick man you can't lose,
I'll get you anything you need.
Keys lids acid and speed.

The Fair in the Woods

to Jere Fransway

The woodsmen blow their horns, and close the day,
Grouped by some logs. The buckskins they are in
Merge with ground's russet and with tree-trunk's grey,
And through the color of the body's skin
Shift borrowings out of nearby birch and clay.

All day a mounted angel came and went
Sturdily pacing through the trees and crowd,
His brown horse glossy and obedient.
Points glowed among his hair: dark-haired, dark-browed.
He supervised a god's experiment.

Some clustered in the upper boughs, from where
They watched the groups beneath them make their way,
Children of light, all different, through the fair,
Pulsing among the pulsing trunks. And they,
The danglers, ripened in the brilliant air.

Upon a platform dappled by the sun
The whole speed-family in a half round clapped
About the dancer where she arched and spun.
They raced toward stillness till they overlapped,
Ten energies working inward through the one.

Landscape of acid:
                              where on fern and mound
The lights fragmented by the roofing bough
Throbbed outward, joining over broken ground

To one long dazzling burst; as even now
Horn closes over horn into one sound.

Knuckle takes back its color, nail its line.
Slowly the tawny jerkins separate
From bark and earth, but they will recombine
In the autumnal dusk, for it is late.
The horns call. There is little left to shine.

LSD, San Rafael Woods: 'Renaissance Fair'

Listening to Jefferson Airplane

in the Polo Grounds, Golden Gate Park

The music comes and goes on the wind,
Comes and goes on the brain.

To Natty Bumppo

The grey eyes watchful and a lightened hand.
The ruder territory opening up
Fills with discovery: unoutlined land
With which familiar places overlap.

A feeling forward, or a being aware.
I reach, out, on: beyond the elm-topped rise
There is, not yet but forming now, a there
To be completed by the opened eyes.

A plain, a forest, a field full of folk.
Footing the sun-shot turf beneath the trees,
They brandish their arms upward like the oak,
Their sky-blue banners rest along the breeze.

Open on all sides, it is held in common,
The first field of a glistening continent
Each found by trusting Eden in the human:
The guiding hand, the bright grey eyes intent.

The Garden of the Gods

All plants grow here; the most minute,
  Glowing from turf, is in its place.
  The constant vision of the race:
Lawned orchard deep with flower and fruit.

So bright, that some who see it near,
  Think there is lapis on the stems,
  And think green, blue, and crimson gems
Hang from the vines and briars here.

They follow path to path in wonder
  Through the intense undazzling light.
  Nowhere does blossom flare so white!
Nowhere so black is earthmould under!

It goes, though it may come again.
  But if at last they try to tell,
  They search for trope or parallel,
And cannot, after all, explain.

It was sufficient, there, to be,
  And meaning, thus, was superseded.
  —Night circles it, it has receded,
Distant and difficult to see.

Where my foot rests, I hear the creak
  From generations of my kin,
  Layer on layer, pressed leaf-thin.
They merely are. They cannot speak.

This was the garden's place of birth:
   I trace it downward from my mind,
   Through breast and calf I feel it vined,
And rooted in the death-rich earth.

Flooded Meadows

In sunlight now, after the weeks it rained,
Water has mapped irregular shapes that follow
Between no banks, impassive where it drained
Then stayed to rise and brim from every hollow.
Hillocks are firm, though soft, and not yet mud.
Tangles of long bright grass, like waterweed,
Surface upon the patches of the flood,
Distinct as islands from their valleys freed
And sharp as reefs dividing inland seas.
Yet definition is suspended, for,
In pools across the level listlessness,
Light answers only light before the breeze,
Cancelling the rutted, weedy, slow brown floor
For the unity of unabsorbed excess.

Grasses

Laurel and eucalyptus, dry sharp smells,
Pause in the dust of summer. But we sit
High on a fort, above grey blocks and wells,
And watch the restless grasses lapping it.

Each dulling-green, keen, streaky blade of grass
Leans to one body when the breezes start:
A one-time pathway flickers as they pass,
Where paler toward the root the quick ranks part.

The grasses quiver, rising from below.
I wait on warm rough concrete, I have time.
They round off all the lower steps, and blow
Like lights on bended water as they climb.

From some dark passage in the abandoned fort,
I hear a friend's harmonica—withdrawn sound,
A long whine drawling after several short . . .
The spiky body mounting from the ground.

A wail uneven all the afternoon,
Thin, slow, no noise of tramping nor of dance.
It is the sound, half tuneless and half tune,
With which the scattered details make advance.

Kirby's Cove

36

The Messenger

Is this man turning angel as he stares
At one red flower whose name he does not know,
   The velvet face, the black-tipped hairs?

His eyes dilated like a cat's at night,
His lips move somewhat but he does not speak
   Of what completes him through his sight.

His body makes to imitate the flower,
Kneeling, with splayed toes pushing at the soil,
   The source, crude, granular, and sour.

His stillness answers like a looking glass
The flower's, it is repose of unblown flame
   That nests within the glow of grass.

Later the news, to branch from sense and sense,
Bringing their versions of the flower in small
   Outward into intelligence.

But meanwhile, quiet and reaching as a flame,
He bends, gazing not at but into it,
   Tough stalk, and face without a name.

Being Born

The tanker slips behind a distant ridge
And, on the blue, a formal S of smoke
Still hangs. I send myself out on my look.
But just beyond my vision, at the edge

To left and right, there reach or seem to reach
Margins, vague pillars, not quite visible,
Or unfleshed giant presences so tall
They stretch from top to bottom, sky to beach.

What memory loosed, of man and boundary blended?
One tug, one more, and I could have it here.
—Yes that's it, ah two shapes begin to clear:
Midwife and doctor faintly apprehended.

I let them both almost solidify,
Their quiet activity bit by bit outlined,
Clean hand and calm eye, but still view behind,
Bright crinkling foam, headland, and level sky.

I think of being grabbed from the warm sand,
Shiny red bawling newborn with clenched eyes,
Slapped into life; and as it clarifies
My friends recede, alas the dwindling land.

Must I rewrite my childhood? What jagg'd growth
What mergings of authority and pain,
Invading breath, must I live through again?
Are they the past or yet to come or both?

Both. Between moving air and moving ocean
The tanker pushes, squat and purposeful,
But elsewhere. And the smoke. Though now air's pull
Begins to suck it into its own motion.

There is a furnace that connects them there.
The metal, guided, cuts through fall and lift,
While the coils from it widen, spread, and drift
To feed the open currents of the air.

At the Center

1

What place is this
                    Cracked wood steps led me here.
The gravelled roof is fenced in where I stand.
But it is open, I am not confined
By weathered boards or barbed wire at the stair,
From which rust crumbles black-red on my hand.
If it is mine. It looks too dark and lined.

What sky
          A pearly damp grey covers it
Almost infringing on the lighted sign
Above Hamm's Brewery, a huge blond glass
Filling as its component lights are lit.
You cannot keep them. Blinking line by line
They brim beyond the scaffold they replace.

2

What is this steady pouring that
                                 Oh, wonder.
The blue line bleeds and on the gold one draws.
Currents of image widen, braid, and blend
—Pouring in cascade over me and under—
To one all-river. Fleet it does not pause,
The sinewy flux pours without start or end.

What place is this
                    And what is it that broods
Barely beyond its own creation's course,
And not abstracted from it, not the Word,
But overlapping like the wet low clouds
The rivering images—their unstopped source,
Its roar unheard from being always heard.

What am
                    Though in the river, I abstract
Fence, word, and notion. On the stream at full
A flurry, where the mind rides separate!
But this brief cresting, sharpened and exact,
Is fluid too, is open to the pull
And on the underside twined deep with it.

3   .

Terror and beauty in a single board.
The rough grain in relief—a tracery
Fronded and ferned, of woods inside the wood.
Splinter and scar—I saw them too, they poured.
White paint-chip and the overhanging sky:
The flow-lines faintly traced or understood.

Later, downstairs and at the kitchen table,
I look round at my friends. Through light we move
Like foam. We started choosing long ago

—Clearly and capably as we were able—
Hostages from the pouring we are of.
The faces are as bright now as fresh snow.

LSD, Folsom Street

The Discovery of the Pacific

They lean against the cooling car, backs pressed
Upon the dusts of a brown continent,
And watch the sun, now Westward of their West,
Fall to the ocean. Where it led they went.

Kansas to California. Day by day
They travelled emptier of the things they knew.
They improvised new habits on the way,
But lost the occasions, and then lost them too.

One night, no one and nowhere, she had woken
To resin-smell and to the firs' slight sound,
And through their sleeping-bag had felt the broken
Tight-knotted surfaces of the naked ground.

Only his lean quiet body cupping hers
Kept her from it, the extreme chill. By degrees
She fell asleep. Around them in the firs
The wind probed, tiding through forked estuaries.

And now their skin is caked with road, the grime
Merely reflecting sunlight as it fails.
They leave their clothes among the rocks they climb,
Blunt leaves of iceplant nuzzle at their soles.

Now they stand chin-deep in the sway of ocean,
Firm West, two stringy bodies face to face,
And come, together, in the water's motion,
The full caught pause of their embrace.

Sunlight

Some things, by their affinity light's token,
Are more than shown: steel glitters from a track;
Small glinting scoops, after a wave has broken,
Dimple the water in its draining back;

Water, glass, metal, match light in their raptures,
Flashing their many answers to the one.
What captures light belongs to what it captures:
The whole side of a world facing the sun,

Re-turned to woo the original perfection,
Giving itself to what created it,
And wearing green in sign of its subjection.
It is as if the sun were infinite.

But angry flaws are swallowed by the distance;
It varies, moves, its concentrated fires
Are slowly dying—the image of persistence
Is an image, only, of our own desires:

Desires and knowledge touch without relating.
The system of which sun and we are part
Is both imperfect and deteriorating.
And yet the sun outlasts us at the heart.

Great seedbed, yellow center of the flower,
Flower on its own, without a root or stem,
Giving all color and all shape their power,
Still re-creating in defining them,

Enable us, altering like you, to enter
Your passionless love, impartial but intense,
And kindle in acceptance round your center,
Petals of light lost in your innocence.

My Sad Captains

part one

The will is infinite
and the execution confined,
the desire is boundless
and the act a slave to limit.

TROILUS AND CRESSIDA

Two Old English words are used in the
twelfth poem: *byrnies* were chain-mail
shirts, and a *nicker* was a water monster.

In Santa Maria del Popolo

Waiting for when the sun an hour or less
Conveniently oblique makes visible
The painting on one wall of this recess
By Caravaggio, of the Roman School,
I see how shadow in the painting brims
With a real shadow, drowning all shapes out
But a dim horse's haunch and various limbs,
Until the very subject is in doubt.

But evening gives the act, beneath the horse
And one indifferent groom, I see him sprawl,
Foreshortened from the head, with hidden face,
Where he has fallen, Saul becoming Paul.
O wily painter, limiting the scene
From a cacophony of dusty forms
To the one convulsion, what is it you mean
In that wide gesture of the lifting arms?

No Ananias croons a mystery yet,
Casting the pain out under name of sin.
The painter saw what was, an alternate
Candor and secrecy inside the skin.
He painted, elsewhere, that firm insolent
Young whore in Venus' clothes, those pudgy cheats,
Those sharpers; and was strangled, as things went,
For money, by one such picked off the streets.

I turn, hardly enlightened, from the chapel
To the dim interior of the church instead,

In which there kneel already several people,
Mostly old women: each head closeted
In tiny fists holds comfort as it can.
Their poor arms are too tired for more than this
—For the large gesture of solitary man,
Resisting, by embracing, nothingness.

The Annihilation of Nothing

Nothing remained: Nothing, the wanton name
That nightly I rehearsed till led away
To a dark sleep, or sleep that held one dream.

In this a huge contagious absence lay,
More space than space, over the cloud and slime,
Defined but by the encroachments of its sway.

Stripped to indifference at the turns of time,
Whose end I knew, I woke without desire,
And welcomed zero as a paradigm.

But now it breaks—images burst with fire
Into the quiet sphere where I have bided,
Showing the landscape holding yet entire:

The power that I envisaged, that presided
Ultimate in its abstract devastations,
Is merely change, the atoms it divided

Complete, in ignorance, new combinations.
Only an infinite finitude I see
In those peculiar lovely variations.

It is despair that nothing cannot be
Flares in the mind and leaves a smoky mark
Of dread.
        Look upward. Neither firm nor free,

Purposeless matter hovers in the dark.

The Monster

I left my room at last, I walked
The streets of that decaying town,
I took the turn I had renounced
Where the carved cherub crumbled down.

Eager as to a granted wish
I hurried to the cul de sac.
Forestalled by whom? Before the house
I saw an unmoved waiting back.

How had she never vainly mentioned
This lover, too, unsatisfied?
Did she dismiss one every night?
I walked up slowly to his side.

Those eyes glazed like her windowpane,
That wide mouth ugly with despair,
Those arms held tight against the haunches,
Poised, but heavily staying there:

At once I knew him, gloating over
A grief defined and realized,
And living only for its sake.
It was myself I recognized.

I could not watch her window now,
Standing before this man of mine,
The constant one I had created
Lest the pure feeling should decline.

What if I were within the house,
Happier than the fact had been
—Would he, then, still be gazing here,
The man who never can get in?

Or would I, leaving at the dawn
A suppler love than he could guess,
Find him awake on my small bed,
Demanding still some bitterness?

The Middle of the Night

Open, box, for the child
Who lifts out, one by one,
Impudent and self-willed
Dolls from the living heap
—Their antics never done
Which took him from his sleep.

Lion and citizen,
Soldier in pose of fight,
A wicker stork, small men,
Small gods and animals . . .
The box is emptied out:
The floor is bright with dolls.

Year after year the same,
A town of perfect size.
Who calls it a mere game?
Round him, alive and shrunk
Each finished burgher lies,
Whose cargoes have been sunk.

He learns their histories—
Jerk, posture, giggle, prance,
And grows to recognize
In each doll, passive, faded,
Some man who is at once
Transfigured and degraded.

At length he writes it down,
Recording what befalls
Until the dark is gone.
Children who know by heart
The vices of their dolls
Will stay awake at night.

Readings in French

1

Refining Mallarmé at last destroyed
Flesh, passion, and their consequent confusions;
His poetry continued in a void
Where only furniture could have illusions.

2

Though Edgar Poë writes a lucid prose,
Just and rhetorical without exertion,
It loses all lucidity, God knows,
In the single, poorly rendered English version.

3

Nothing Unusual about Marcel Proust
All are unmasked as perverts sooner or later,
With a notable exception—the narrator.

4

L'Education Sentimentale
Mme Arnoux is finely never there.
That is the point: the fineness, the despair.

5

Nausea fills me, and the only essence
Is in my tangible illegal presence.
I start from here. But where then did I learn
The terms that pose the choices I discern?

From the Highest Camp

Nothing in this bright region melts or shifts.
The local names are concepts: the Ravine,
Pemmican Ridge, North Col, Death Camp, they mean
The streetless rise, the dazzling abstract drifts,
To which particular names adhere by chance,
From custom lightly, not from character.
We stand on a white terrace and confer;
This is the last camp of experience.

What is that sudden yelp upon the air?
And whose are these cold droppings? whose malformed
Purposeless tracks about the slope? We know.
The abominable endures, existing where
Nothing else can: it is—unfed, unwarmed—
Born of rejection, of the boundless snow.

Innocence

for Tony White

He ran the course and as he ran he grew,
And smelt his fragrance in the field. Already,
Running he knew the most he ever knew,
The egotism of a healthy body.

Ran into manhood, ignorant of the past:
Culture of guilt and guilt's vague heritage,
Self-pity and the soul; what he possessed
Was rich, potential, like the bud's tipped rage.

The Corps developed, it was plain to see,
Courage, endurance, loyalty and skill
To a morale firm as morality,
Hardening him to an instrument, until

The finitude of virtues that were there
Bodied within the swarthy uniform
A compact innocence, childlike and clear,
No doubt could penetrate, no act could harm.

When he stood near the Russian partisan
Being burned alive, he therefore could behold
The ribs wear gently through the darkening skin
And sicken only at the Northern cold,

Could watch the fat burn with a violet flame
And feel disgusted only at the smell,
And judge that all pain finishes the same
As melting quietly by his boots it fell.

Modes of Pleasure

I jump with terror seeing him,
Dredging the bar with that stiff glare
As fiercely as if each whim there
Were passion, whose passion is a whim:

The Fallen Rake, being fallen from
The heights of twenty to middle age,
And helpless to control his rage,
So mean, so few the chances come.

The very beauty of his prime
Was that the triumphs which recurred
In different rooms without a word
Would all be lost some time in time.

Thus he reduced the wild unknown.
And having used each hour of leisure
To learn by rote the modes of pleasure,
The sensual skills as skills alone,

He knows that nothing, not the most
Cunning or sweet, can hold him, still.
Living by habit of the will,
He cannot contemplate the past,

Cannot discriminate, condemned
To the sharpest passion of them all.
Rigid he sits: brave, terrible,
The will awaits its gradual end.

Modes of Pleasure

New face, strange face, for my unrest.
I hunt your look, and lust marks time
Dark in his doubtful uniform,
Preparing once more for the test.

You do not know you are observed:
Apart, contained, you wait on chance,
Or seem to, till your callous glance
Meets mine, as callous and reserved.

And as it does we recognize
That sharing an anticipation
Amounts to a collaboration—
A warm game for a warmer prize.

Yet when I've had you once or twice
I may not want you any more:
A single night is plenty for
Every magnanimous device.

Why should that matter? Why pretend
Love must accompany erection?
This is a momentary affection,
A curiosity bound to end,

Which as good-humored muscle may
Against the muscle try its strength
—Exhausted into sleep at length—
And will not last long into day.

A Map of the City

I stand upon a hill and see
A luminous country under me,
Through which at two the drunk must weave;
The transient's pause, the sailor's leave.

I notice, looking down the hill,
Arms braced upon a window sill;
And on the web of fire escapes
Move the potential, the grey shapes.

I hold the city here, complete:
And every shape defined by light
Is mine, or corresponds to mine,
Some flickering or some steady shine.

This map is ground of my delight.
Between the limits, night by night,
I watch a malady's advance,
I recognize my love of chance.

By the recurrent lights I see
Endless potentiality,
The crowded, broken, and unfinished!
I would not have the risk diminished.

The Book of the Dead

The blood began to waste into the clods.
Meanwhile his soldiers kept the dead away
At sword-point, though some clamored by the gods,
And some by friendship—hard, hard to deny.

Slowly the form took body; they could see
Blood flow down the diaphanous throat, slow, stay,
Clot, till the neck became opaque. And he,
Tiresias, stood before them, heavy as they.

What comfort could he bring them? (Circling past,
Poor, drained of cunning, they would also grope
After a goat's blood even.) Might the last
Action of which he spoke be ground for hope?
But winnowing is one action out of many.
After the winnowing, you must grind, bake, eat,
And then once more turn out into the rainy
Acres to plow, your mantle weighing wet
Round your swaddled ankles, your knuckles raw, your cheek
Fretted with tiny veins,—and not assured
That it will be, this time, either easier work
Or more successful. Even, perhaps, more hard.

Yet by the time Odysseus saw the throat,
Guttering, whiten, he was glad. The dead
Desire what they can never bring about;
The living bring discriminate gifts of blood,
Clumsily, wasting far more than they give,

But able still to bring. He knew the lack,
And watching, without comfort, was alive
Because he had no comfort. He turned back.

The Byrnies

The heroes paused upon the plain.
When one of them but swayed, ring mashed on ring:
    Sound of the byrnie's knitted chain,
Vague evocations of the constant Thing.

They viewed beyond a salty hill
Barbaric forest, mesh of branch and root
    —A huge obstruction growing still,
Darkening the land, in quietness absolute.

That dark was fearful—lack of presence—
Unless some man could chance upon or win
    Magical signs to stay the essence
Of the broad light that they adventured in.

Elusive light of light that went
Flashing on water, edging round a mass,
    Inching across fat stems, or spent
Lay thin and shrunk among the bristling grass.

Creeping from sense to craftier sense,
Acquisitive, and loss their only fear,
    These men had fashioned a defense
Against the nicker's snap, and hostile spear.

Byrnie on byrnie! as they turned
They saw light trapped between the man-made joints,
    Central in every link it burned,
Reduced and steadied to a thousand points.

Thus for each blunt-faced ignorant one
The great grey rigid uniform combined
   Safety with virtue of the sun.
Thus concepts linked like chainmail in the mind.

   Reminded, by the grinding sound,
Of what they sought, and partly understood,
   They paused upon that open ground,
A little group above the foreign wood.

Black Jackets

In the silence that prolongs the span
Rawly of music when the record ends,
   The red-haired boy who drove a van
In weekday overalls but, like his friends,

   Wore cycle boots and jacket here
To suit the Sunday hangout he was in,
   Heard, as he stretched back from his beer,
Leather creak softly round his neck and chin.

   Before him, on a coal-black sleeve
Remote exertion had lined, scratched, and burned
   Insignia that could not revive
The heroic fall or climb where they were earned.

   On the other drinkers bent together,
Concocting selves for their impervious kit,
   He saw it as no more than leather
Which, taut across the shoulders grown to it,

   Sent through the dimness of a bar
As sudden and anonymous hints of light
   As those that shipping give, that are
Now flickers in the Bay, now lost in night.

   He stretched out like a cat, and rolled
The bitterish taste of beer upon his tongue,
   And listened to a joke being told:
The present was the things he stayed among.

If it was only loss he wore,
He wore it to assert, with fierce devotion,
   Complicity and nothing more.
He recollected his initiation,

   And one especially of the rites.
For on his shoulders they had put tattoos:
   The group's name on the left, The Knights,
And on the right the slogan Born To Lose.

Baudelaire among the Heroes

Charles Baudelaire knew that the human heart
Associates with not the whole but part.
The parts are fetishes: invariable
Particularities which furnish hell.

The Value of Gold

The hairs turn gold upon my thigh,
And I am gold beneath the sun,
Losing pale features that the cold
Pinched, pointed, for an instant I
Turn blind to features, being one
With all that has, like me, turned gold.

I finish up the can of beer,
And lay my head on the cropped grass:
Now bordering flag, geranium,
And mint-bush tower above me here,
Which color into color pass
Toward the last state they shall become.

Of insect size, I walk below
The red, green, greenish-black, and black,
And speculate. Can this quiet growth
Comprise at once the still-to-grow
And a full form without a lack?
And, if so, can I too be both?

I darken where perpetual
Action withdraws me from the sun.
Then from one high precocious stalk
A flower—its fullness reached—lets fall
Features, great petals, one by one
Shrivelling to gold across my walk.

Claus von Stauffenberg

of the bomb plot on Hitler, 1944

What made the place a landscape of despair,
History stunned beneath, the emblems cracked?
Smell of approaching snow hangs on the air;
The frost meanwhile can be the only fact.

They chose the unknown, and the bounded terror,
As a corrective, who corrected live
Surveying without choice the bounding error:
An unsanctioned present must be primitive.

A few still have the vigor to deny
Fear is a natural state; their motives neither
Of doctrinaire, of turncoat, nor of spy.
Lucidity of thought draws them together.

The maimed young Colonel who can calculate
On two remaining fingers and a will,
Takes lessons from the past, to detonate
A bomb that Brutus rendered possible.

Over the maps a moment, face to face:
Across from Hitler, whose grey eyes have filled
A nation with the illogic of their gaze,
The rational man is poised, to break, to build.

And though he fails, honor personified
In a cold time where honor cannot grow,
He stiffens, like a statue, in mid-stride
—Falling toward history, and under snow.

part two

I looked back as we crossed the crest of the foothills—with the air so clear you could see the leaves on Sunset Mountains two miles away. It's startling to you sometimes—just air, unobstructed, uncomplicated air.

The Last Tycoon
F. SCOTT FITZGERALD

PART TWO

Waking in a Newly Built House

The window, a wide pane in the bare
modern wall, is crossed by colorless
peeling trunks of the eucalyptus
recurring against raw sky-color.

It wakes me, and my eyes rest on it,
sharpening, and seeking merely all
of what can be seen, the substantial,
where the things themselves are adequate.

So I observe them, able to see
them as they are, the neutral sections
of trunk, spare, solid, lacking at once
disconnectedness and unity.

There is a tangible remoteness
of the air about me, its clean chill
ordering every room of the hill-
top house, and convoking absences.

Calmly, perception rests on the things,
and is aware of them only in
their precise definition, their fine
lack of even potential meanings.

Flying above California

Spread beneath me it lies—lean upland
sinewed and tawny in the sun, and

valley cool with mustard, or sweet with
loquat. I repeat under my breath

names of places I have not been to:
Crescent City, San Bernardino

—Mediterranean and Northern names.
Such richness can make you drunk. Sometimes

on fogless days by the Pacific,
there is a cold hard light without break

that reveals merely what is—no more
and no less. That limiting candor,

that accuracy of the beaches,
is part of the ultimate richness.

Considering the Snail

The snail pushes through a green
night, for the grass is heavy
with water and meets over
the bright path he makes, where rain
has darkened the earth's dark. He
moves in a wood of desire,

pale antlers barely stirring
as he hunts. I cannot tell
what power is at work, drenched there
with purpose, knowing nothing.
What is a snail's fury? All
I think is that if later

I parted the blades above
the tunnel and saw the thin
trail of broken white across
litter, I would never have
imagined the slow passion
to that deliberate progress.

"Blackie, the Electric Rembrandt"

We watch through the shop-front while
Blackie draws stars—an equal

concentration on his and
the youngster's faces. The hand

is steady and accurate;
but the boy does not see it

for his eyes follow the point
that touches (quick, dark movement!)

a virginal arm beneath
his rolled sleeve: he holds his breath.

. . . Now that it is finished, he
hands a few bills to Blackie

and leaves with a bandage on
his arm, under which gleam ten

stars, hanging in a blue thick
cluster. Now he is starlike.

Hotblood on Friday

Expectant yet relaxed, he
basks within the body's tight
limits, the tender reaches;
and acquires by street-light the
details which accumulate
to a sense of crude richness

that almost unseats reason.
At last, the present! His step
springs on the sidewalk like a
voice of appetite. The town
is gradually opening up,
this as on every Friday:

stone petals bright in the warm
evening. No hand can grasp it.
Quick, Hotblood, in the boisterous
community find some term,
precarious and accurate,
that assumes it without loss.

The Feel of Hands

The hands explore tentatively,
two small live entities whose shapes
I have to guess at. They touch me
all, with the light of fingertips

testing each surface of each thing
found, timid as kittens with it.
I connect them with amusing
hands I have shaken by daylight.

There is a sudden transition:
they plunge together in a full
formed single fury; they are grown
to cats, hunting without scruple;

they are expert but desperate.
I am in the dark. I wonder
when they grew up. It strikes me that
I do not know whose hands they are.

L'Épreuve

for Paul Bowles

I

My body trots semblably
on Market Street. I control
that thick and singular spy
from a hovering planet: I
contemplate new laws meanwhile.

According to which it is
not a thoroughfare below
but a sweet compact. I choose
as if for the first time this
as the world I'll come back to.

II

Not yet. I am distinct. I
am now afflicted with thirst,
heat and cold, bombarded by
rockets that explode greenly,
harried by shapes, cramped. The worst

is, I am still on my own.
The street's total is less near
during my long ordeal than
the turbanned legends within
my world of serried color.

Rastignac at 45

Here he is of course. It was his best
trick always: when we glance again toward
the shadow we see it has consist-
ed of him all along, lean and bored.

We denounced him so often! Yet he
comes up, and leans on one of the bars
in his dark suit, indicating the
empty glass as if we were waiters.

We fill it, and submit, more or less,
to his marvellous air of knowing
all the ropes debonair weariness
could care to handle, of "everything

that I know I know from having done,
child, and I survive." What calmly told
confidences of exploration
among the oversexed and titled,

or request for a few days' loan, are
we about to hear? Rastignac tell us
about Life, and what men of your
stamp endure. It must be terrible.

It is. To the left of his mouth is
an attractive scarlike line, not caused
by time unhelped. It is not the prize,
either, of a dueller's lucky thrust.

But this: time after time the fetid
taste to the platitudes of Romance
has drawn his mouth up to the one side
secretly, in a half-maddened wince.

We cannot help but pity him that
momentary convulsion; however,
the mere custom of living with it
has, for him, diminished the horror.

Lights among Redwood

And the streams here, ledge to ledge,
take care of light. Only to
the pale green ribs of young ferns
tangling above the creek's edge
it may sometimes escape, though
in quick diffusing patterns.

Elsewhere it has become tone,
pure and rarefied; at most
a muted dimness colored
with moss-green, charred grey, leaf-brown.
Calm shadow! Then we at last
remember to look upward:

constant, to laws of size and
age the thick forms hold, though gashed
through with Indian fires. At once
tone is forgotten: we stand
and stare—mindless, diminished—
at their rosy immanence.

of Muir Woods

Adolescence

After the history has been made,
and when Wallace's shaggy head

glares on London from a spike, when
the exiled general is again

gliding into Athens harbor
now as embittered foreigner,

when the lean creatures crawl out of
camps and in silence try to live;

I pass foundations of houses,
walking through the wet spring, my knees

drenched from high grass charged with water,
and am part, still, of the done war.

A Trucker

Sometimes it is like a beast
barely controlled by a man.
But the cabin is lofty
as a skull, and all the rest
extends from his foot as an
enormous throbbing body:

if he left anything to
chance—see his great frame capsize,
and his rubber limbs explode
whirling! and see there follow
a bright fountain of red eyes
tinkling sightless to the road.

Loot

I am approaching. Past dry
towers softly seeding from mere
delicacy of age, I
penetrate, through thickets, or

over warm herbs my feet press
to brief potency. Now with
the green quickness of grasses
mingles the smell of the earth,

raw and black. I am about
to raid the earth and open
again those low chambers that
wary fathers stand guard in.

II

Poised on hot walls I try to
imagine them caught beneath
in the village, in shadow:
I can almost hear them breathe.

This time what shall I take? Powers
hidden and agile, yield now
value: here, uniquely yours.
Direct me. But dark below

in the boneworks, you only
move in time with my pulse, and
observe without passion the
veer of my impassioned mind.

III

This. Hands numb from sifting soil
I find at last a trinket
carved whole from some mineral:
nameless and useless thing that

is for me to name and use.
But even as I relax my
fingers round its cool surface,
I am herald to tawny

warriors, woken from sleep, who
ride precipitantly down
with the blood toward my hands, through
me to retain possession.

My Sad Captains

One by one they appear in
the darkness: a few friends, and
a few with historical
names. How late they start to shine!
but before they fade they stand
perfectly embodied, all

the past lapping them like a
cloak of chaos. They were men
who, I thought, lived only to
renew the wasteful force they
spent with each hot convulsion.
They remind me, distant now.

True, they are not at rest yet,
but now that they are indeed
apart, winnowed from failures,
they withdraw to an orbit
and turn with disinterested
hard energy, like the stars.